Howard B. Wigglebottom
Listens to His Heart

Written by

Howard Binkow

Illustrated by

Susan F. Cornelison

Written by: Howard Binkow
Illustrated by: Susan F. Cornelison
Book design by: Tobi S. Cunningham

Thunderbolt Publishing
We Do Listen Foundation
www.wedolisten.com

This book is the result of a joint creative effort with Ana Rowe and Susan F. Cornelison.

Gratitude and appreciation are given to all those who reviewed the story prior to publication.
The book became much better by incorporating several of their suggestions.

Rhonda J. Armistead, Karen Binkow, Peggy Brooks, Principal Brian S. Buchanan, Deborah Cochran, Adria de Haume, Mikki Doh,
Sandra Duckworth, Susie Eden, Lillian Freeman, Sarah Garrison, Terrylee Gauvin, Jan Marie Guinn, Martha Gutierrez, Jennifer Guldalian,
Amy Hamilton, Kerry Harr, Stephanie Herrero, Sherry L. Holland, Stacy Jensen, Tracy Mastalski, Teri Poulos, Chris Primm, Sharon Purser,
Laurie Sachs, Mimi Savio, C. J. Shuffler, Nancey Silvers, Gayle Smith, Pam Smith, Joan Sullivan, Phyliss Steinberg,
Rosemary Underwood, Terri Veach, George Sachs Walor, Robyn Hart Williams, and Susanne Wilt

Teachers, librarians, counselors, and students at:

C. Hunter Ritchie Elementary School, Warrenton, Virginia
Central Maine Preschool, Cornville, Maine
Charleston Elementary School, Charleston, Arkansas
Evaluation Center Bossier Parish Schools, Bossier City, Louisiana
Florida-Kansas Elementary School, Memphis, Tennessee
Glen Alpine Elementary, Morganton, North Carolina
Golden West Elementary School, Manteca, California
Iveland Elementary, St. Louis, Missouri
J. L. Mulready School, Hudson, Massachusetts
Mary Lou Dieterich School, Modesto, California

Meadows Elementary, Manhattan Beach, California
Patterson Primary School, Beaver Falls, Pennsylvania
Plaza Towers Elementary, Moore, Oklahoma
Robert Frost Elementary, Westerville, Ohio
Sherman Oaks Elementary, Sherman Oaks, California
Washington-Franklin Elementary, Farmington, Missouri
West Navarre Primary, Navarre, Florida
Wheelock Primary School, Fredonia, New York
Williard F. Prior Elementary School, Oneida, New York

Special thanks to my family for their ideas and support and to the After-School Pop Stars™, Cortland Tate-Kerecz,
Marcela Barry, and Zoe Himmel.

Third printing, January 2010
Printed in Shenzen, China by Asia Pacific Offset

ISBN: 978-0-9715390-8-2

This book belongs to

_____

Learn more about Howard in our award-winning first book
Howard B. Wigglebottom Learns to Listen.

Howard B. Wigglebottom used to LOVE to dance!

Whenever Howard felt sad, he would dance
and wiggle away the blues.

Dancing **ALWAYS** made him happy!

HEE

Until one day at school when the other kids made fun of him . . .

8

Hee Hee Ha Ha Ha Ha Ho
Hee Hee Hee Hee Ha Ha Ha Ho Ho Ho
Hee Hee Ha Ha Ho Ho Ho

. . . and the dancing STOPPED!

Howard wanted to fit in. Being liked and acting cool was important—so important that he decided he would . . .

NEVER DANCE AGAIN!

"Maybe everyone will like me if I'm a rock star, so I think I'll try singing!" Howard said to himself.

. . . But that didn't go quite as planned.

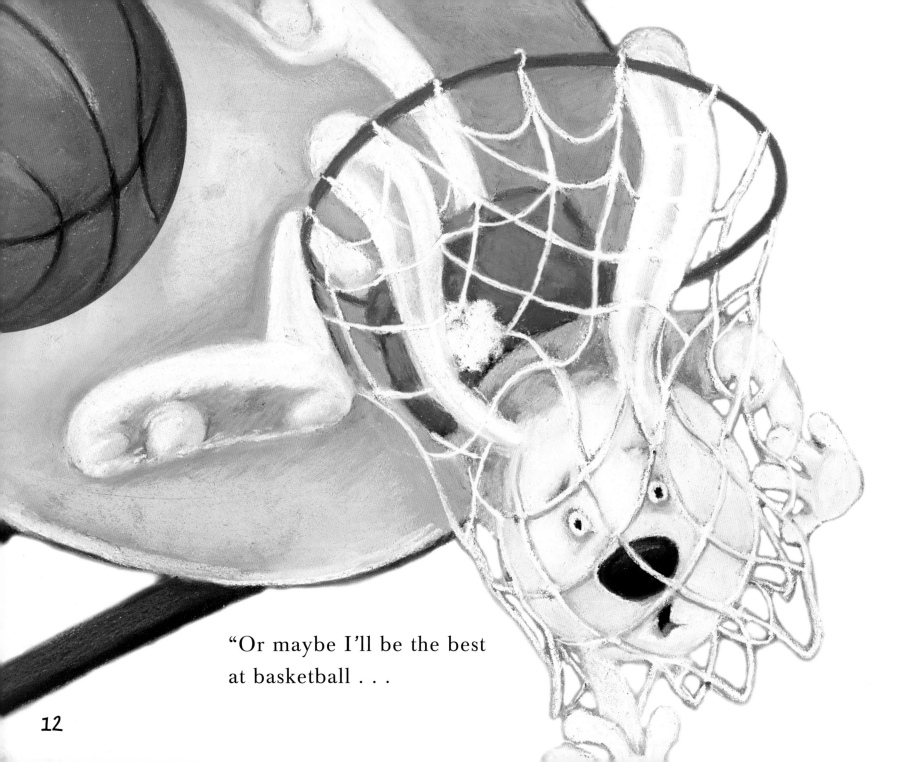

"Or maybe I'll be the best at basketball . . .

12

. . . Or maybe art. Then I'll be liked for sure."

Howard felt everyone was better than he was and that there must be something wrong with him.

Just when it seemed his day couldn't get any worse . . .

. . . IT DID!
After school, Howard's little sister hopped by and said, "I'll race you home." Howard tried his hardest, but he knew he wasn't really that fast for a rabbit.

Grandpa Sammy could see his little
grandson was a changed bunny.
His "wiggle" was gone.

"What's wrong, Howard?"
he asked.

"Nothing," Howard mumbled.

"That's not what I see,"
said Grandpa. "It's okay.
You can tell me. I'm a
good listener."

Howard told Grandpa everything. "I keep trying and trying, and I'm not good at anything. There must be something wrong with me," Howard cried.

"There's nothing wrong with you, Howard. You're good enough just as you are," said Grandpa. "Try doing things just for the fun of it, for what you'll learn, and for the friends you'll meet along the way.

"It's not about winning or being liked. Listen to your heart. Do things that make you feel good, no matter what your friends say.

"What makes you feel really good?"

Howard answered **"DANCING**!
I love to dance, Grandpa."

18

"I thought so," Grandpa said. "If you like dancing, then practice and be the best dancer you can be.

"Maybe I can help. I know a thing or two about dancing. I used to wiggle a bit in my day. Dancing goes way back in our family.

"Howard, you come from a long line of Wigglebottoms," added Grandpa.

Every day after school, Grandpa Sammy taught
Howard new dance moves!

Howard's favorite dance was the one he made up all by himself. And he and Grandpa called it "The Wigglebottom."

21

One day Grandpa said, "Howard, be proud of yourself for doing your best and trying different moves. You listened to your heart and invented your very own dance. And now, I can tell you feel really good inside."

But the next morning when Howard read the school poster,

SOCK HOP DANCE AFTER SCHOOL THIS FRIDAY,

he became nervous. Howard wanted to go, but what if his friends laughed at him AGAIN!

Friday arrived, and everyone gathered in the gym after school.

The music started.

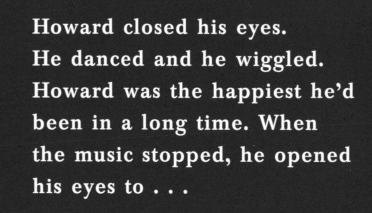

Howard closed his eyes.
He danced and he wiggled.
Howard was the happiest he'd
been in a long time. When
the music stopped, he opened
his eyes to . . .

silence.

But what he heard next made his heart sing. One person started clapping, then another, and another. Soon everyone was yelling and cheering, "You **ROCK**, Howard! **AWESOME**! You're the **BEST**! Teach us your cool moves, Howard."

Howard smiled from ear to ear. There was a joy in Howard's heart that he hadn't felt in a long time. **DANCING MADE HIM FEEL REALLY GOOD INSIDE**!!! He was proud to be who he was born to be—a Wigglebottom through and through.

Howard B. Wigglebottom Listens to His Heart
Suggestions for Lessons and Reflection

1. The Heart

★ There are two different meanings for the word *heart*. One is that the heart is a muscle that pumps blood through the whole body. The other is when people talk about their feelings and they say things like "You broke my heart," "Listen to your heart," "There is joy in your heart," "You make my heart sing," "My heart stopped," "Sweetheart," or "I love you with all my heart."

★ When you are asked to follow your heart, it means to do things you really like and that make you feel good inside. Following your heart, listening to your heart, and being true to yourself mean the same thing. When you listen to your heart, you will be proud of the decisions you make and the person you are.

★ In our first book, *Howard B. Wigglebottom Learns to Listen,* Howard learns how to listen to his teachers and parents. In this book, Howard learns how to listen to his heart, which is the same as listening to himself and doing what is right for him.

★ Do you know the difference between *to think* and *to feel*? Examples of thoughts are, "He's not nice." or "He's smart." Examples of feelings are "I feel sad." or "I feel happy."

★ Can you think of anyone like Howard who followed his heart even when his friends made fun of him?

2. Confiding In an Older Person

★ Howard was very lucky to have a grandfather he trusted to talk about his feelings. In addition to your parents, find someone older you trust and are comfortable with to share your feelings. It may be a brother, a sister, a nice teacher, a nurse, or a doctor.

3. Self-Esteem, Inclusion, and Acceptance

★ As human beings, we all have the same needs. First, we need to eat, breathe, drink, sleep, be liked, and be heard. Next, we belong to smaller groups called *races*. Do you know which race you belong to? One can be a mixture of different races. Races look different from one another. Then you belong to an even smaller group called *family*. Every family is different, and every family member is unique. You have a different age, feelings, needs, thoughts, tastes, desires, and talents. It's okay to be different. Do you know what makes you different from the rest of your family?

★ As an individual person, you need to find out what you like and what makes you happy. As you meet other children, you'll find out the differences in them and how they may become your friends. There will be times when what makes your friends happy will be different from what makes you happy. It's not easy to accept that your friends may have likes and dislikes that are different from yours. It's not easy to feel different from your friends and still feel liked by everyone.

* Do things that you like, and you will have a better chance to meet friends who will accept and like you as you are and enjoy doing the things you like to do.

* You are good enough just as you are. It's okay to be yourself and not what others may want you to be. Remember to say to yourself everyday, "I am special."

* All of us have the ability to find out what we like to do best.

* Howard got cheers and compliments for finding what he loved to do and for trying his hardest. Sometimes you will get cheers and sometimes you won't. It doesn't matter whether you get cheers or not. What's important is that you do those things you believe in and that make you feel good.

* If you do things that you don't like just to look cool to your friends, you will not feel good inside.

* It's okay not to be perfect in everything you do. As long as you don't give up and always do your best, you can feel good about yourself. And you will be proud of yourself too!

4. Trying Different Things for the Fun of It

* It's a good idea to try different things—even ones you don't like very much. Why? Because:

    you will find out more about what you like and your own talents.

    you will make good friends who like you as you are.
    you will feel proud and good about yourself.
    you will learn many different things that you will get to use all your life, even when you are a grown-up.

* Do you know of anyone like Howard who tried many different things until he found something that made his heart sing?

5. Connecting to Your Roots and Family Legacy

* In the story, Howard learns about the talents he received from his family from a really long time ago. What did it mean when Grandpa Sammy said "You, Howard, come from a long line of Wigglebottoms?"

* Often, we don't share the same talents or gifts as our parents. And that's okay. In the story, Howard does share a talent with his family. What talent does he share with other Wigglebottoms?

* Would you like to learn what gifts you may have received from your family from a long time ago? Ask someone about your family history. If you can't find out anything, learn about the history of your race.

* **BE PROUD OF WHO YOU ARE !!**

31

Learn more about Howard's other adventures.

Books

Howard B. Wigglebottom Learns to Listen

Howard B, Wigglebottom Learns About Bullies

Howard B. Wigglebottom Learns About Mud and Rainbows

Visit www.wedolisten.com.
Enjoy free Howard B. Wigglebottom animated books, songs, games, activities, lessons, posters, and E Cards.

You may email the author at howardb@wedolisten.com.

Comments and suggestions are appreciated.